D1517655

J

BEECHWOOD BUNNY TALES

MISTLETOE
and the Baobab Tree

Beechwood Bunny Tales
Dandelion's Vanishing Vegetable Garden
Mistletoe and the Baobab Tree
Periwinkle at the Full Moon Ball
Poppy's Dance

Library of Congress Cataloging-in-Publication Data

Huriet, Geneviève.
  [Mistouflet Passiflore et le baobab. English]
  Mistletoe and the baobab tree / written by Geneviève Huriet ;
illustrated by Loïc Jouannigot.
      p. cm. — (Beechwood bunny tales)
  Translation of: Mistouflet Passiflore et le baobab.
  Summary: After spending the day searching for the fabled baobab tree,
Mistletoe the rabbit learns to appreciate the warmth and comfort of his
own home.
    ISBN 0-8368-0527-5
  [1. Explorers—Fiction. 2. Rabbits—Fiction.] I. Jouannigot, Loïc, ill. II.
Title. III. Series.
PZ7.H95657Mi   1991   [E]—dc20   90-46856

North American edition first published in 1991 by
Gareth Stevens Children's Books
1555 North RiverCenter Drive, Suite 201
Milwaukee, Wisconsin 53212, USA

English text by MaryLee Knowlton

Printed in the United States of America

 2 3 4 5 6 7 8 9 95 94 93 92 91

BEECHWOOD BUNNY TALES

MISTLETOE
and the Baobab Tree

written by GENEVIÈVE HURIET   illustrated by LOÏC JOUANNIGOT

Gareth Stevens Children's Books
MILWAUKEE

It was a hot summer day in Beechwood Grove. The Bellflower bunnies had finished their gardening long before the heat rose. Now they were resting in the coolness of the house.

Papa Bramble, Aunt Zinnia, and even little Dandelion slept peacefully. Poppy, Violette, and Periwinkle quietly played cards. Only Mistletoe was busy. He filled his flask, stuffed carrots in his pack, and looked for his hat.

Periwinkle heard the commotion in the next room and looked up from the card game.

"Where are you going, Mistletoe?" he asked. The other bunnies stopped playing and looked up, too.

"I'm off to explore the desert!" Mistletoe answered.

"There's no desert around here," said Poppy.

"Oh, yes there is!" Mistletoe insisted. "I've found it."

"Take us with you, then," the bunnies chorused.

"Not today," replied Mistletoe. "I have exploring on my mind." And off he went in the direction of the big valley.

Just beyond Beechwood Grove ran a small river. The summer heat had shrunk the river to a tiny trickle, leaving a plain of rubble and sand where nothing grew. This was Mistletoe's desert.

Mistletoe loved this adventure. He jumped the tiny stream and climbed among the rocks, whistling and humming happily. He never imagined he could be bothering anyone.

A cranky heron named Harry stood quietly nearby, trying to catch fish for his family. At the sound of Mistletoe's merry whistle, the fish took off for quieter parts. Harry was annoyed.

With long, stiff steps, he approached Mistletoe. "Hey, noisy Nellie, what are you doing here?"

"Why, I'm exploring the desert," Mistletoe answered timidly. A sly grin slid across the crafty heron's face.

"Well, you'd better keep moving if you're going to explore the way the great explorers do," Harry said, his eyes gleaming.

"How is that?" asked Mistletoe. "I do want to do it right."

"Well, then," replied Harry, beginning to enjoy his trick, "you'll have to go from here to follow the river to the foot of the baobab tree. You know, big trunk, few leaves. You'll want to sit in its shade like all the great explorers do."

"I'm on my way," Mistletoe called excitedly. And with that, he set off briskly under the noonday sun.

Oh, but it is hard work crossing the desert at midday. Poor Mistletoe thought he would melt away as he stumbled over rocks and floundered in the sand. But all the while, he scanned the horizon for the baobab tree.

At last, far ahead, Mistletoe sighted a tree. It had a thick trunk and a few branches hung with brown leaves. Mistletoe had found the baobab tree! His explorer's heart beat faster.

With great effort, he dragged himself to the tree. And there, with his chin held proudly, he sat awhile just like the explorers of old. All he needed was someone to witness his great feat.

But wait! There were witnesses! Above Mistletoe's head perched three black crows.

"What is that?" one crow asked.

"It's a rabbit!" answered another.

"What is he doing here?" asked the third. But no one could answer that.

Mistletoe made a grand gesture. "I have crossed the great desert to sit in the shade of the baobab tree," he said proudly.

The three crows cawed loudly. "Where do you think you are — Africa?" they laughed, nearly falling from their branch. "This is an oak tree — a nearly dead one at that."

And with that they flew off, their laughter swirling arour Mistletoe like the desert heat.

Alone now, Mistletoe looked around. Yes, his baobab tree was just an old oak tree. And the desert, well, it looked like an old riverbed. As he tried to muster his spirit, he noticed the long shadows. He must get home before dark.

Sadly, he looked at his blistered paws and his empty pack. Just enough of his explorer's spirit returned to help him choke back the tears, and he started for home. He trudged slowly, with his shoulders slumped sadly and his head bowed. This would be a long, long walk.

Suddenly, he heard a familiar voice. "Mistletoe! Mistletoe!" It was Papa!

"Over here!" the tired bunny called. "I'm coming! I'm coming!" But Papa found him before he had gone much farther.

Papa was very glad to see Mistletoe, but did he scold! "What were you thinking of, Mistletoe? This is madness! In this heat!"

Mistletoe tried to feel sorry, but he was just too glad to be going home on Papa's back to feel bad.

The sun had already set when Papa arrived home with
Mistletoe. Aunt Zinnia snatched up the tired bunny and
popped him into bed with a cold compress on his head.

"I wish I had seen the real baobab tree," Mistletoe
murmured as he drifted off to sleep.

When Mistletoe awoke the next day, everyone gathered around to hear his story. But he didn't want to talk about it and turned over to sleep again. He noticed a picture at the end of his bed, signed by Poppy, which showed two lions and a large, odd-looking tree.

"I copied it from the dictionary," Poppy said shyly.

Mistletoe's spirits began to rise. "May I have a pencil, please?" he asked.

As the family watched, Mistletoe drew a rabbit with a backpack and three crows. Between the two lions, he drew a sneaky heron. Finally, beneath the strange tree, he wrote: "Baobab."

As Mistletoe finished drawing, his brothers and sister "oohed" and "aahed." Their faces glowed with excitement. Well, Mistletoe thought, maybe his adventure had been a success after all.